W9-CGM-132

Bubble Blowers, Beware!

adapted by David Lewman
illustrated by Barry Goldberg

based on the movie written by Derek Drymon, Tim Hill,
Steve Hillenburg, Kent Osborne, Aaron Springer, and Paul Tibbitt

SCHOLASTIC INC.
New York Toronto London Auckland Sydney
Mexico City New Delhi Hong Kong Buenos Aires

Stephen Hillenburg

Based on *The SpongeBob SquarePants Movie* created by Nickelodeon Movies and Paramount Pictures

ISBN 0-439-66695-3

12 11 10 9 8 7 6 5 4 3 2 1   4 5 6 7 8 9/0

Printed in the U.S.A.

First Scholastic printing, November 2004

"See, Patrick?" asked SpongeBob. "This is the Patty Wagon!"

Patrick licked his lips. "Can I eat it now?"

"No, we're going to drive it to Shell City and find King Neptune's crown," explained SpongeBob.

"But I thought you didn't have a driver's license," said Patrick.

"You don't need a license to drive a sandwich," answered SpongeBob.

As they drove toward Shell City, SpongeBob and Patrick sang their favorite song. *"I'm a Goofy Goober, yeah!"* bellowed Patrick.

Soon they were out of gas.

"What'll it be—ketchup or mustard?" asked a gas station attendant. He slapped his thigh, laughing hard at his own joke.

SpongeBob smiled. "This car runs on high-octane unleaded. The mustard goes in the windshield washer tank."

The gas station attendant laughed even harder.

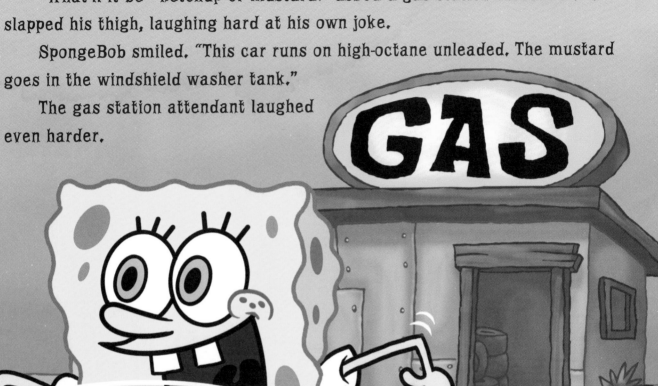

"Where are you two kids headed?" the attendant asked between snorts of laughter.

"We two *men* are going to Shell City to get King Neptune's crown back," explained SpongeBob, making his voice as deep as possible.

The attendant laughed even more. "Shell City! You two won't last ten seconds over the county line!"

As soon as SpongeBob and Patrick crossed the county line a tough-looking thug stopped them.

"Out of the car, fellas," he said.

SpongeBob and Patrick got out and watched the thug drive away in the Patty Wagon.

"How long was that?" SpongeBob asked the gas station attendant.

"Twelve seconds," he answered.

"All right!" shouted SpongeBob happily.

The attendant shook his head. "They're doomed," he muttered.

"Are we there yet?" whined Patrick. They'd been walking for what seemed like hours.

SpongeBob spotted a sign. "That says Shell City is only three . . . thousand miles away," he sighed. "We'll never make it in time. If only we still had the Patty Wagon."

Suddenly Patrick pointed ahead. "Look!" he cried.

SpongeBob saw a tough-looking pool hall. Parked next to it was a huge sandwich.

It was their Patty Wagon!

SpongeBob and Patrick ran over to the Patty Wagon. But when they looked inside the key wasn't there.

SpongeBob peeked through a window of the pool hall and saw the thug who had taken the Patty Wagon. The key was attached to his belt.

"How are we going to get the key?" asked Patrick.

SpongeBob had an idea. "I'll go in and create a distraction. Then you get the key!"

"Ooh, wait! I want to do the distraction!" pleaded Patrick.

"Okay," said SpongeBob. "I guess it doesn't really matter who does the distraction."

Patrick rushed over to the door and SpongeBob followed.

Patrick threw open the doors and strode into the pool hall. SpongeBob sneaked in behind him.

"Can I have everybody's attention?" yelled Patrick.

The music stopped. All the tough guys in the pool hall turned and glared at Patrick.

"I have to use the bathroom," he said.

The thug who had taken the Patty Wagon said, "It's right over there." Patrick hurried into the bathroom.

Then the thug looked down at SpongeBob, who was trying to take the key off his belt. SpongeBob giggled nervously. "Oh, right," he said. "The bathroom . . . that's, uh, what I'm looking for too."

SpongeBob burst into the bathroom. "Patrick, you call that a distraction?!"

Patrick shrugged. "I had to go to the bathroom."

"That guy's belt was filthy," grumbled SpongeBob. "I got my hands dirty for nothing."

He walked to the sink and pumped the soap dispenser. A bunch of perfect bubbles floated out. "Hey, Patrick," called SpongeBob. "Check it out—bubbles!"

"Bubble party!" they whooped.

But then they heard an angry voice outside the door. "WHO BLEW THIS BUBBLE?" it growled.

"All right," said the pool hall manager. "You all know the rule."

The tough guys stopped playing pool and spoke at the same time. "Anyone who blows a bubble will be laughed at by every able-bodied person in the pool hall."

SpongeBob and Patrick peeked out the bathroom door to see what was going on.

"Right!" roared the manager. "So, who blew that bubble? Someone in here is just a kid, not a real man."

SpongeBob and Patrick tried to sneak out the back door, but the manager spotted them. "YOU TWO! COME HERE!"

The manager grabbed SpongeBob and Patrick. He made them line up with the other thugs.

"We're looking for a bubble blower," he said. "And don't think we don't know how to find 'em. No kid can resist singing along to this song."

When the song began, Patrick trembled. "SpongeBob," he whispered. "It's the Goofy Goober theme song!"

"I know," whispered SpongeBob. "Don't sing along!"

The manager turned the music up louder. Patrick opened his mouth and took a deep breath.

"Patrick!" hissed SpongeBob. "Don't . . . sing . . . along!"

"I'm trying," said Patrick. "Trying so hard!"

Patrick was just about to crack. He couldn't resist singing along to his favorite song in the world! SpongeBob trembled. He was sure Patrick was about to sing when all of a sudden . . .

"I'm a Goofy Goober, yeah!" Two Siamese twin fish started singing the song!
"Which one of you two kids did it?" the manager yelled. The twin fish
pointed at each other. "It was him," they said at the same time.

All the thugs laughed at the twin fish.

During the confusion SpongeBob and Patrick slipped out to the parking lot.

SpongeBob wiped his brow. "Whew, that was a close call."

He saw the Patty Wagon still sitting there. "But we still don't have the key," he said sadly. He walked over to the big sandwich and patted its hood. "We'll never make it to Shell City. I guess we really are just a couple of kids."

Patrick walked up to SpongeBob. He had a funny look on his face. "Yup, we're just a couple of kids . . ."

". . . who got the key!" Patrick whipped his hand out from behind his back. He was holding the key to the Patty Wagon!

"Patrick, that's fantastic!" said SpongeBob.

They jumped into the Patty Wagon. SpongeBob turned the key and they sped off toward Shell City to get Neptune's crown.

And as they drove they sang,

"I'm a Goofy Goober, yeah!"